Fancy NANCY

There's No Day Like a Snow Day

Based on *Fancy Nancy* written by Jane O'Connor

Cover illustration by Robin Preiss Glasser

Interior illustrations by Carolyn Bracken

HARPER FESTIVAL
An Imprint of HarperCollins Publishers

HarperFestival is an imprint of HarperCollins Publishers.

Fancy Nancy: There's No Day Like a Snow Day
Text copyright © 2012 by Jane O'Connor
Illustrations copyright © 2012 by Robin Preiss Glasser

www.harpercollinschildrens.com
Library of Congress catalog card number: 2012934237
ISBN 978-0-06-208629-7
Book design by Sean Boggs
12 13 14 15 16   CWM   10 9 8 7 6 5 4 3 2
❖
First Edition

Ooh la la! It started snowing last night and now it's a blizzard! The radio says this is the storm of the century—a century is a fancy way of saying a hundred years.

"All the schools are closed," I announce to my parents.
Then I call Bree with the joyful news. "Come over *tout de suite!*"
(That's French for "right away." You say it like this—toot sweet.)

"Nancy, it's only six thirty," my mom says. "Bree can come over after breakfast when Mrs. DeVine comes to babysit."

"Oh, no! You mean you have to go to work? On a snow day?"

"Grown-ups don't get snow days," my dad says. "That is a sad but true fact of life."

I feel so sorry for my parents that I make them a special treat for breakfast. "Look! It's snowing on your cereal," I say as I sprinkle shredded coconut into their bowls.

JoJo and I get all bundled up...

...and drag our sleds out of the garage. We are ready to frolic!
(Frolic is fancy for having fun.)

At last! Mrs. DeVine arrives with Bree and Freddy.
"Can we go to Mount Everest right away?" I ask. Mount Everest
is what everybody calls the biggest hill in the park. The sledding there
is phenomenal, which means fabulous, spectacular, and totally
awesome!

"Darling, I'm afraid my sledding days are long over. I want all of you to stay in the yard where I can see you. I'll supervise from inside."

No sledding? We are all *très, très* disappointed, but I remind everyone that there are many other ways to frolic on a snow day.

First we make snow angels. We decorate the wings with pinecones.

Can you guess what I'm doing now? I bet you think I
am building a snowman. But you are sadly mistaken,
which means you are wrong, wrong, wrong!

I get a bunch of accessories from my room and...

voilà! Here is our snow king, snow queen, snow princess, and snow prince. Don't they look regal? That's a fancy word for royal.

We all bow and curtsy, because that is what you're supposed to do in front of royalty.

Soon we hear Mrs. DeVine calling us to come inside.

Ooh la la! Hot chocolate with mini marshmallows. And there are plates of Mrs. DeVine's delectable homemade cookies. Each one looks like a snowflake. "Merci!" I say. "What a thoughtful thing to do."

It is twilight now, which is a lovely word for when it's almost dark out. We all catch snowflakes on our tongues and wait for our parents to get home.

When Mom and Dad get home, they tell us how sorry they are to have missed all the fun.

"But there's still time for more frolicking," I point out. "We haven't gone sledding yet. Can we go now?" I am almost positive the answer will be no, but—double ooh la la!—they say, "Why not!" So we pile the sleds into the cars and off we go to Mount Everest.

Soon we are zooming down the hill at supersonic speed. That means really, really fast! Do you know what is just as much fun as a snow day?

A snow night!

Make your own royal snow family!